*Library of Congress Catalog-in-Publication
Data*: Berenstain, Stan, 1923-
The Berenstain Bears' sampler : the best of
Bear Country / by Stan & Jan Berenstain.
  p. cm.—(First Time Books)
CONTENTS: New baby—The sitter—In the
dark—Go to the doctor—The messy room
ISBN: 0-679-87790-8
[1. Bears—Fiction. 2. Stories in rhyme.]
I. Berenstain, Jan,1923- . II. Title.
III. Series: Berenstain, Jan, 1923- . First
Time Books. PZ8.3.B4493Bhs 1995
[E]—dc20   95-465

The Berenstain Bears'

SAMPLER

THE BEST OF BEAR COUNTRY

Stan & Jan Berenstain

Random House 🏠 New York

Compilation copyright © 1995 by Berenstains, Inc.
The Berenstain Bears and the Messy Room copyright © 1983 by Berenstains, Inc. The Berenstain Bears and the Sitter copyright © 1981 by Berenstains, Inc. The Berenstain Bears Go to the Doctor copyright © 1981 by Berenstains, Inc. The Berenstain Bears in the Dark copyright © 1982 by Berenstains, Inc. The Berenstain Bears' New Baby copyright © 1974 by Stanley and Janice Berenstain.

Manufactured in the United States of America   10 9 8 7 6 5 4 3 2 1

The Berenstain Bears'
NEW BABY

This way to Bear Country
You'll know when you're there
As soon as you enter
You'll feel like a bear

Down a sunny dirt road, over a log
bridge, up a grassy hill, deep in Bear
Country, lived a family of bears—
Papa Bear, Mama Bear and Small Bear.

They lived in a large tree
which Papa Bear had hollowed out
and made into a house.

It was a very fine house.
This is what it looked like inside.

It was fun growing up in Bear Country . . .

helping Papa get honey from the old bee tree . . .

helping Mama bring the vegetables
in from the garden.

There were all sorts of interesting things for a small bear to do and see in Bear Country.

Small Bear felt good growing up
in a tree . . . in his own room . . . in the
snug little bed that Papa Bear had made
for him when he was a baby.

But one morning, it did not feel
so good. Small Bear woke up with
pains in his knees and aches in his legs.

"Small Bear, you have outgrown
your little bed," said Papa Bear, as he
hitched up his overalls and buttoned
his shoulder straps.

"Today, we shall go out into the woods and make you a bigger one!"

With that, he ate his
breakfast of piping-hot
porridge ...

washed it down with a
gulp of honey from the
family honey pot ...

took up his ax and was
out the door.

"But, Papa," called
Small Bear, following
after him. "What will
happen to my little bed?"

"Don't worry about that,
Small Bear," said Mama Bear
as she closed the door after him.

She smiled and patted her
front, which had lately grown
very big and round.
"You've outgrown
that snug little bed
just in time!"

"What will happen to my little bed?" Small Bear asked as he caught up with Papa Bear. But Papa was sharpening his ax on his grinding stone and didn't hear.

"Yes, indeed," said Papa Bear. "You need a bed you can stretch out in—a bed that will not give you pains in your knees and aches in your legs."

He tested
the ax to see
if it was sharp,

then headed off
into the woods.

"What will happen to my little bed?"
Small Bear asked again as he caught up with
Papa Bear in the woods. Papa had chopped
down a tree and was splitting it into boards.
"We will have a new baby soon
who will need that little bed,"
said Papa Bear as he whacked
off another board.

"A new baby?" asked Small Bear.
(He hadn't noticed that Mama Bear had
grown very round lately, although he
had noticed it was harder and harder
to sit on her lap.)

"And it's coming soon?"

"Yes, *very* soon!" said Papa Bear.

With a final whack he split off the last
board, which gave him enough wood to make
a bigger bed for Small Bear.

They made the bed a good size
and took the rest of the day to
chip and shave it smooth and neat.
Then they carried it back to
the tree and up to Small Bear's room.

When they got there,
Small Bear noticed right away
that his old bed wasn't there
any more.

"My little bed!" said
Small Bear. "It's already
gone!"

"You outgrew it just in time,"
called Mama Bear from the next room.
"Come and see."

It was true! There was his snug
little bed with a new little baby in it.
Small Bear had outgrown his snug
little bed just in time for his new baby
sister. And now *he* was a *big brother!*

She was very little but very
lively. As Small Bear leaned over
for a closer look, she popped him
on the nose with a tiny fist.

"Hmm," said Small Bear. "She
has a pretty good punch for a little baby."

That night he stretched out
proudly in his bigger bed.
"Aah!" he said. "Being a
big brother is going to be fun."

The next morning he woke up feeling fine,
with no pains in his knees or aches in his legs.
His nose was a little tender, though.

The Berenstain Bears
and the
SITTER

Mom and Dad are going out,
Gramps and Gran are, too.
Who will stay home
with the cubs?
Just anyone won't do…

"What's this?" said Papa Bear, as he took the day's mail from the Bear Family's mailbox.

It was a notice telling about an important meeting that night at the Bear Country Town Hall.

Mama Bear called up Grizzly Gran. Brother and Sister Bear sometimes stayed with Gramps and Gran when Mama and Papa Bear had to be away.

But Gramps and Gran were planning to go to the meeting, too. So Brother and Sister couldn't stay with them.

Or with Aunt Maude . . .

or Cousin Wilbur.
They were going to the
meeting, too.

"Why can't we go with you?" asked Sister, beginning to get a little upset.

"Yeah!" added Brother Bear.

"Because," said Papa, "this meeting is for grown-ups. And, besides, it won't be over until late—way past your bedtime."

"Well, where are we going to stay?" the cubs wanted to know.

"You're going to stay right here,"
said Mama, as she put down the phone.
"Alone?" asked Sister.
"Of course not," said Mama.
"I've arranged for a sitter."
"A sitter?!" said Brother.
"Who is it going to be?"
Sister asked.
"Mrs. Grizzle, who lives
in the hollow stump at the
end of the road," said Mama,
feeling much better about
the whole thing.

"Mrs. Grizzle!" said the
cubs, not feeling better
at all. . . .

Once, when Sister was playing with her friends, their ball went into Mrs. Grizzle's flower garden.
Mrs. Grizzle wasn't too happy about it.

And another time, when Brother was flying his kite, it swooped and bumped Mrs. Grizzle on the hat.

She wasn't too tickled about that, either.

Later that evening, after the supper things
had been cleaned up, Mama and Papa got ready to
go to the town meeting.

"But who's going to scrub our backs, read us a
story, and tuck us in?" asked Sister, still a little
nervous about the idea of a sitter.

"I understand that Mrs. Grizzle has raised
seven cubs of her own," said Mama, putting on her
hat. "And I'm sure she's a perfectly good back
scrubber, story reader, and tucker-inner."

"She's not going to scrub *my* back!"
Brother Bear said under his breath.

Mrs. Grizzle came walking up the path to the Bears' tree house right on time.

There was no question about it. It was the same Mrs. Grizzle who got bopped with the kite and didn't like cubs tromping her flowers.

She was very large—almost as big as Papa— and she carried a drawstring bag.

"Evenin', all!" said Mrs. Grizzle in a loud, jolly voice. "Well, time's a-wastin', you two!" she said to Mama and Papa. "You better skedaddle off to your meetin'!"

Mrs. Grizzle had a strong way of saying things, and folks usually did what she said.

Mama and Papa kissed the cubs good night—and skedaddled.

"Whew!" said Mrs. Grizzle, as she sat down in Papa's big chair. "It sure is good to get a load off your feet!" She took off her hat and looked into her drawstring bag.

There's something about somebody looking into a bag that makes cubs very curious.

"Mrs. Grizzle?" said Sister.

"Yes?"

"What's in the bag?"

"Nothin' much. Just some things I take along when I go sittin'—a piece of string, a pack of cards . . ."

Meanwhile, over at the Town Hall, the bears were getting ready for their important meeting.

They were getting ready for speeches, voting, and arguments about some new laws.

But Mama's mind was not on the meeting. Neither was Papa's. Mama and Papa Bear were thinking about what was going on back home.

"Sister looked a little worried when we left," fretted Mama.

"So did Brother," agreed Papa.

They decided to call home and see how things were going.

"Things are goin' just fine," said Mrs. Grizzle. "Brother and Sister can't come to the phone right now. They're busy playin' Cat's Cradle. . . . "

"Have a good meeting!" shouted the cubs.

"—But they say to have a good meetin'!"

After Cat's Cradle, they played Go Fish with the cards that came out of Mrs. Grizzle's drawstring bag.

Then they played Tiddly-winks with a special set of winks that Mrs. Grizzle had made out of polished stones and a snail-shell cup.

After a while, the cubs got the yawns, and Mrs. Grizzle began getting them ready for bed.

And she did, indeed, turn out to be a very good back scrubber (Brother changed his mind about not having his back scrubbed)....

And she was
a fine story reader . . .

and a really super
tucker-inner.

The cubs had a number of different sitters
from time to time, but Mrs. Grizzle was their
favorite—and they were always glad to see her.

The Berenstain Bears
IN THE DARK

Being afraid
of the dark
Doesn't just happen
to you.
It happens,
sometimes,
To little bears, too.

Sister and Brother Bear were at the Bear Country Library. Sister had already chosen her books and was waiting at the check-out desk.

"Hold your horses," said Brother. "I'm looking for a good mystery."

Sister Bear usually took out storybooks and books about nature—and sometimes books of poems. Brother liked those, too, but lately he'd become interested in mysteries—especially spooky ones.

"Hey, this one looks good," he said finally. "Okay, let's check out."

"Hmmm," said Sister, looking at the cover. It was called *The Case of the Crying Cave.* "It looks scary to me!"

"Say! This is really good!"
said Brother later that
evening when the Bear family
had settled down for some
reading. "Would you like me to read
it to you?" he asked Sister.

Sister was looking at a storybook
about three kittens who were arguing
about which was the prettiest—
and it *was* a little boring.

"Or are you scared?" teased Brother.
"Of course not," said Sister. She left
her book on the floor and climbed onto
the bench to sit beside him.

The mystery began quietly. It told
about some bear scouts who were on
an overnight camp-out.

"A mysterious cave!" said the bear scouts. "We should explore it!"

But before the scouts could go into the cave a wailing sound came from the cave.

WHOOOOOO

It was a strange sound and it frightened the scouts. "Help!" they cried.

OO-OO-O

When the scouts discovered a dark, secret cave, Brother's mystery began to get a little exciting. And when the cave began to cry and wail, it was anything but quiet!

"'*Who-o-o-o-o!* cried the deep, dark mysterious cave,'" read Brother with a lot of expression. "'*Who-o-o-o-o!*'"

"Stop!" said Sister, putting her fingers in her ears. "That's enough!" And she went back to her storybook.

"Scaredy bear! Scaredy bear!" teased Brother.

"And that's quite enough of *that*," added Papa Bear, looking up from his paper.

At the cubs' bedtime Papa and Mama said good night, turned off the light, and left the cubs in the usual sleepy darkness.

Outside the tree house the bright, busy sounds of day had given way to the soft, soothing sounds of night—the quiet conversation of frogs and toads, the soft cry of the owl, the sigh of the night wind. And if you listened very hard, you could *almost* hear the softest sound of all—the sound of lightning bugs switching their lights on and off, on and off.

But inside the tree house Sister Bear wasn't even beginning to fall asleep. That night the dark didn't seem the least bit quiet and sleepy. In fact, it seemed like the spooky darkness of a scary cave. And the friendly old chest of drawers and funny clothes tree that Papa had made didn't seem so friendly and funny. They seemed more like cave creatures.

So when Brother decided to tease her a little more by making a wailing noise—a really spooky wailing noise— it gave her quite a scare.

"Mama! Papa!" she cried. "Hurry! Come quick!"

And come quickly they did.

Papa rushed into the dark room and tripped over the clothes tree.

Mama rushed in after Papa and tripped over him.

In the commotion Sister fell out of bed and landed on both of them!

Then Brother, who had started it all with his spooky wail, turned on the light. What a mess! Sister, still scared, was holding on to Papa. Papa was holding on to the toe he had stubbed. And Mama was looking for the nightcap she had lost in the confusion. All three of them were pretty annoyed with Brother Bear.

It turned out to be a very
long night in the Bears' tree
house. Papa and Mama tried to
explain that there was nothing
to be afraid of in the dark
(except maybe running into a
clothes tree and stubbing your
toe)—but it didn't do any good.

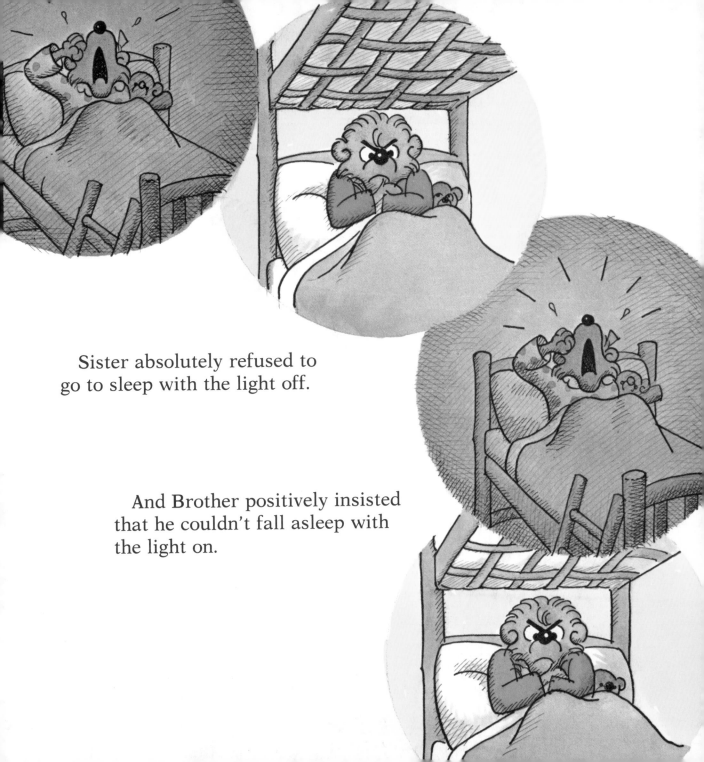

Sister absolutely refused to go to sleep with the light off.

And Brother positively insisted that he couldn't fall asleep with the light on.

The next morning the Bear family was very sleepy-eyed.
"Boy," said Brother, yawning, "I sure don't want to go through another night like that!"
"Neither do I," said Papa. "And I think I have an idea that might help."

He took Sister's hand. "Come with me," he said.

"Where are we going?" she wanted to know.

"Up to the attic."

"The attic? But it's dark in the attic—even in the daytime."

"I know," said Papa. "But there's something I want to show you. Anyway, there's nothing so special about the dark. It's just part of nature, like the light. It's your imagination that makes the dark seem spooky sometimes."

"What's imagination?" asked Sister.

"Imagination is what makes us think that chests of
drawers and clothes trees are cave creatures."

"I wish I didn't have one," said Sister.

"Don't say that," said Papa. "A lively imagination
is one of the best things a cub can have. It's
imagination that lets us paint pictures, make up
poems, invent inventions! The trick is to take charge
of your imagination—and not let it take charge of you."

When they got to the attic, Papa began to rummage through boxes, looking for something.

Sister tried to follow Papa's advice and not let her imagination take charge.

And it worked—a spooky shape turned out to be the shadow of some old tools.

What looked like a giant was really some piled-up furniture.

"Here it is!" said Papa. "My old night light!
The one I used when I was a cub and had a little
trouble falling asleep in the dark!"

Sister couldn't quite believe that her big,
powerful papa was ever afraid of the dark.

"Oh, sure," said Papa. "Most of us are at one
time or another."

"How about reading the rest of *The Case of the Crying Cave*?" Sister asked Brother later that day.

"Are you sure you want me to?"

"Sure! I want to see how it turns out!" she insisted.

When it turned out that there was nothing very
spooky about the terrible wailing noise (it was
caused by wind blowing across an opening in the
roof of the cave—like the noise you make when
you blow across the top of a bottle), Sister
was a little disappointed.

And that night, when she and Brother were all settled down in the cozy glow of Papa's old night light, she said so. "I was pretty disappointed by the way *The Case of the Crying Cave* ended."

"Why?" asked Brother.

"Because," she said, "I was hoping the wailing would be a really spooky, scary monster!" And she leaned down from her bunk over Brother's and made a spooky, scary monster face at him.

"Cut that out!" cried Brother.

Then Sister went right to sleep.
But Brother lay awake for quite some time
listening to the owl hoots and thinking that
maybe he'd had enough mysteries for a while.

The Berenstain Bears
GO TO THE DOCTOR

Take a deep breath.
Stick out your tongue.
Come see Doctor Grizzly
While you are young.

"Tomorrow," said Mama Bear as she helped the cubs get ready for bed, "you'll be going to the doctor for a checkup."

"Doctor?" said Brother Bear. "We're not sick!"

"And what's a checkup?" asked Sister Bear, a little worried.

"It's just what it sounds like," said Mama. "Dr. Grizzly will check to see if you are growing the way healthy cubs should."

"Will it hurt?"
asked Sister, pulling
the covers up close.

"Now, now," said Papa Bear as he kissed her good night. "You just settle down. There's absolutely nothing to worry about."

But Sister wasn't so sure.

The next morning, after a good breakfast, the family got into their red roadster and were on their way.

"Do you ever get checkups, Mama?"
Sister asked as they drove along the
dusty dirt road.

"Yes, I do," answered Mama.

"*I* don't need checkups anymore," bragged Papa. "Because I . . . I . . .

—AH-CHOO

never get sick."

"That was quite a sneeze,"
said Mama.

"It's this dusty road," said
Papa, turning onto the main
highway into Beartown.

They pulled to a stop in front of the
doctor's office.

"Come, cubs!" said Mama. "We don't want
to be late for our appointment."

But Brother held back. He remembered
something.

G.GRIZZLY M.D.

"Are we going to get shots?" he asked.

"That's up to . . . to . . . to . . .

—AH CHOO!

. . . the doctor," said Papa, sneezing an even bigger sneeze than before.

"Bless you!" said Mama. "It's just this bright sunlight," sniffed Papa. "I *never* get sick."

The doctor's waiting room was a busy, cheerful place with pictures on the walls, books to look at, and puzzles to do. Brother started a puzzle. Sister took a book, but didn't really look at it. Other bears were coming in—and she looked around the room at them. There were cubs of all ages with their parents.

Some of the smallest cubs looked a little worried. Sister smiled at them so they wouldn't be afraid.

There was a big cub with a cast on his leg. It had names and funny drawings all over it.

He let Brother write his name on it for luck, and Sister drew a picture.

There was even a little baby cub only a few weeks old.

"Next!" called Dr. Grizzly. It was Brother's and Sister's turn.

Dr. Grizzly was friendly, but she got right down to work. She had a lot of bears to take care of and not much time to waste.

First, she weighed and measured the cubs.

"Fine!" she said. "You've both gained weight nicely, and grown taller."

She listened to their chests with a stethoscope.

And poked them all over to check on everything inside.

Then, Dr. Grizzly took
each cub's temperature
to see if it was normal . . .

—ninety-eight point six.

She checked their throats.

Then, she looked at their eyes,

ears,

and noses with a
special little light.

Next, she tested their hearing
by whispering very softly.

Then came the eye test. Brother read every letter except the very smallest. Sister didn't know all the letters yet, so she read a special chart that looked like this:

"Very good!" said the doctor, as she studied some papers in a folder.

Sister whispered to Brother, "So far, it hasn't hurt at all!"

"Well, that pretty much takes care of it," said
Dr. Grizzly, looking through her eyeglasses
at the papers, "except for one thing. I see it's time for
your booster shots."

"I knew it!" said Brother.

"Why do we have to have shots when we're not even
sick?" said Sister.

"Now, Sister," said Papa, "the doc . . . doc . . . doc . . .
AH-CHOO! . . . doctor knows best!"

"Bless you," said Dr. Grizzly. "And that's a very
good question, Sister. . . . "

As she got the shots ready, she called out into the
waiting room, "I've got a brave little cub in here who's
going to show you all how to take a shot!"

"Getting back to your question, Sister," said Dr. Grizzly. "You see, there are some kinds of medicine that you take after you get sick, and those are very useful. But this kind of shot is a special medicine that keeps you from *getting* sick."

"Will it hurt?" asked Sister.

"Not nearly as much as biting your tongue or bumping your shin," the doctor explained. "There! All done!"

Dr. Grizzly was right! And it happened so fast that Sister didn't even have time to say ouch!

The little cubs who were watching were *very* impressed.

So was Brother.

After Brother's shot, Papa said, "Well, Doctor, we'll be go . . . go . . . go . . .

—going now."

"Just a minute, Papa Bear," said Dr. Grizzly.
"Let me have a look at you."
"But, I *never* get sick. . . ." Papa started to say.

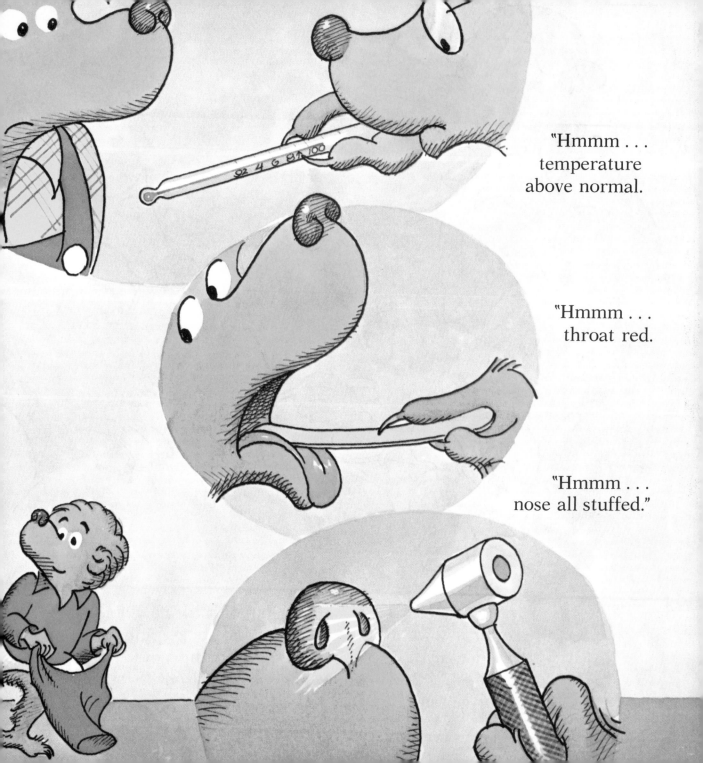

"Hmmm . . .
temperature
above normal.

"Hmmm . . .
throat red.

"Hmmm . . .
nose all stuffed."

"Time for your medicine, Papa!" said the cubs, offering him a big spoonful of the gooey pink stuff that Dr. Grizzly prescribed for his cold.

"Well," said Papa, smiling weakly, "I *hardly* ever get sick!"

The Berenstain Bears and the MESSY ROOM

When small bears forget
To pick up, store and stash,
Some of their favorite things
End up in the trash.

From the outside, the Bears' tree house, which stood beside a sunny dirt road deep in Bear Country, looked very neat and well-kept.

The flower beds sparkled with red, yellow, and blue tulips.

The woodwork was freshly painted and in good repair.

The grass was cut and the vegetable patch was properly weeded.

Even the bird's nest that perched on one of the tree house branches was well-trimmed.

The inside of the Bears'
tree house was neat and clean too.

The pictures were straight.

The piano was dusted.

The kitchen was spick-and-span.

Even the basement was neat and clean.
(And if you think it's easy to keep a
tree house basement neat and clean—
well, you've never tried to do it!)

Yes, the Bears' tree house was a lesson in neatness and cleanliness.

Except for one place...

Brother Bear and Sister Bear's room. IT...WAS...A...*MESS*!!!

A dust-catching, wall-to-wall, helter-skelter mess!

A half-done jigsaw puzzle gathered dust in one corner of the room.

A group of Brother's dinosaur models collected cobwebs in another.

Sister's stuffed animals were everywhere.

It wasn't that Brother and Sister were naturally messy. They *tried* to keep their room straight.

They made their beds...

most of the time,

and they swept
and picked up...

once in a while.

The trouble was that when clean-up time came, they spent more time arguing than cleaning.

"How am *I* supposed to sweep with your dumb dinosaur toys all over the floor?" argued Sister.

"They're not toys—they're *models*! And don't move them! I'm working on a set-up of the Pleistocene Age!" Brother protested.

"Pleistocene schmeistocene!" shouted Sister.

Not only was Brother and Sister's room a mess, but Brother and Sister were getting to be a mess too—always arguing about clean-up chores instead of sharing the job and working as a team.

What usually happened was that while the cubs
argued about whose turn it was to do what,
Mama took the broom and did the sweeping herself...

and she often did the picking up too.
That was the worst part—the picking up.

And the putting away.

Well, the mess just seemed to build up and build up, until one day...maybe it was because Mama's back was a little stiff, or maybe it was stepping on Brother's airplane cement, or maybe she was just fed up with that messy room, but whatever it was...Mama Bear lost her temper!

She stormed into the
cubs' room with a big box.

"The first thing we have to do is get rid of all this junk!" she said.

"JUNK!?" said Brother and Sister, watching in horror as Mama began to throw things into the box.

"My Teddy isn't junk!" screamed Sister.

"My bird's nest collection isn't junk!" yelled Brother at the top of his lungs.

The screaming and yelling got so loud that it reached Papa, who was in his workshop putting the finishing touches on a batch of chairs that had been ordered by one of his customers. He couldn't imagine what was wrong.

He hurried up the stairs and looked into the messy, *noisy* room. It didn't take a deep thinker to figure out what was going on.

Papa got Mama's and the cubs'
attention and called a family meeting
right then and there.

"Now, the mess has really built up in this
room," he said. "In fact, it's the worst case
of messy build-up I've ever seen!
"And it isn't fair," he continued. "It isn't
fair to your mama and me, because we have a lot
of other things to take care of. And it isn't
fair to you, because you really can't have fun
or relax in a room that's such a terrible mess."

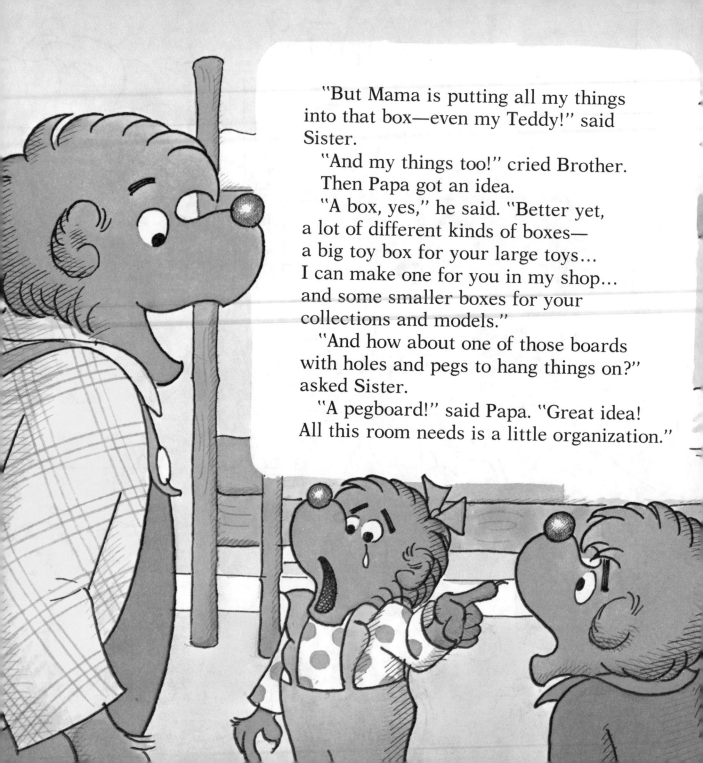

"But Mama is putting all my things into that box—even my Teddy!" said Sister.

"And my things too!" cried Brother. Then Papa got an idea.

"A box, yes," he said. "Better yet, a lot of different kinds of boxes—a big toy box for your large toys... I can make one for you in my shop... and some smaller boxes for your collections and models."

"And how about one of those boards with holes and pegs to hang things on?" asked Sister.

"A pegboard!" said Papa. "Great idea! All this room needs is a little organization."

"A little organization—*and* a few rules!" added Mama. "Rules about more sweeping and less arguing and not leaving things to gather dust and cobwebs."

Papa set to work making
a fine big toy box and a
large pegboard...

while the cubs and Mama
sorted out toys, books, games,
and puzzles and put them
into boxes that fit neatly
into the closet.
Every box was
clearly labeled.

Some of the cubs' things did end up in Mama's big throwaway box— not Sister's Teddy, of course, but some of Brother's bird's nests (the crumbling, falling-apart ones).

It was a very big job cleaning up all that messy build-up. But after a lot of straightening up and putting away, the job was finally finished.

"Wow!" said Brother. "That was quite a job, but it was worth it!"

"It looks like a whole new room!" said Sister.

The cubs were right.

TOYS

And Papa had been right too. It was so much more enjoyable to live in a neat, clean, well-organized room— and so much more relaxing!

It wasn't as exciting to open the big storage closet now, but it was much more practical—and a lot more fun!